The Magical Eggs on Dragon's Lair

GINA SANO

Library of Congress Control Number   2012979221
ISBN: Softcover   978-1-950425-26-6
               eBook   978-1-950425-27-3

Liber Publishing House
www.liberpublishing.com
Hotline: 3158201714

visit: www.sanobooks.com.au
email: booksbysano@gmail.com

Quantity sales. Special discounts are available on quantity purchases by corporations, associations, and others. For details, contact the publisher at above information.

Other books by Gina Sano:

Leap Frog

The Twisted Hickory
Dickory Dock
(also available in Spanish)

The Twisted Hichory
Dickory Dock 2

NORTHVILLE

WESTPIT

EASTPIT

SOUTHVILLE

N
W — E
S

DRAGON'S LAIR

Chapter 1

In faraway land called Pottie is a large island in the middle of a lake. The lake was called Dragon Lake and the island was called Dragon's Lair.

The island itself was shaped like a diamond where two towns were built. The town in the north was called Northville and, you guessed it, the town in the south was called Southville. On the coastline between the two towns were ferry ports. These port villages didn't have much in the way of shops but were the main ferry ports for the island. From eastern port, called Eastpit, people caught the ferry to the airport on the mainland. The western port, called Westpit, the ferry took the people to a forest in the national park, where they could walk the trails to see beautiful landscapes and all sorts of animals.

In Southville, lived the Smith family. The father was called Tom. Tom worked in a factory on the mainland. The factory made fireworks. The mother was caller Mary. Mary worked two days a week in a factory which made glitter. Tom and Mary have two children, twins called Evette and Adam.

Adam and Evette went to the school, the only school on Dragon's Lair. The school, like other important buildings, was in the centre of the island.

At home Evette and Adam were well-behaved. They did their chores like making their beds and keeping their room tidy and that included vacuuming. They helped with setting the table and placing their dishes in the dishwasher. But at school, they were not always well-behaved.

At school, they sometimes teased the other children, ate bits of food from other people's plates or packed lunches after eating everything in front of them. They would also try to sneak a sip of other people's drinks when they had finished their own. Only John who was Adam's only friend and Jane who was Evette's only friend would share a table with the twins. They knew the food and drink pinching were done on purpose to see what and how the other children would say or do. The twins never stole food from either Jane or John. After a while, other children wouldn't even sit near a table close to the twins.

In the classroom, they were slightly better behaved but would always, as they say, 'borrow' other children's equipment and then 'forget' to return them. The teacher had no choice but to sit the twins beside each other and then slightly away from the others. This helped a bit until the twins decided to hum and whisper songs just loud enough for the other children to hear but not always by the teacher.

Now it was school holidays. When both parents were at work, they were taken over to their grandparents', Steve and Sally, home in Eastpit. Tom would drop them off before catching the ferry to the factory on the mainland. Mary would pick them up in the afternoon at four o'clock when she finished her shift at the glitter factory. Adam and Evette didn't always like going to their grandparents' home. There wasn't much to do and when they had their afternoon nap, that time was super boring.

Daytime television had the same cartoons repeated every school holiday. There were no computer games and their parents, Tom and Mary didn't let them take their tablets. The tablets were only for school lessons and homework.

In the past, they would let the chickens out of the chicken run and leave them run wild in the grandparents' garden. When the grandparents woke up, they would laugh at them chasing the hens back into the run. Now that was taken away. The grandparents placed padlocks on the chicken run gate.

Now they were at the grandparents' house again. This time their grandfather, Steve, took them down to the beach at Eastpit. After watching a few ferries come and go from the mainland, Steve took them on a long beach walk to the cliffs which plunged down into the lake. They rested on a rock and drank water and nibbled on fruit and cupcakes.

Chapter 2

Steve asked Adam and Evette, "Do you know how the island and lake got their names?" Both shook their heads. He smiled and lean forward. "Haven't they told you at school?" The twins shook their heads again.

"Oh, dear. It is so important to know how this place got its name. Well, I better tell you."

He took another sip of his water and gave a soft burp. The twins chuckled.

"Long ago, well over 1000 years ago, this place was inhabited by dragons. The two groups of dragons never got on well. There were always fights. Most times their fights would be short lived and things would settle again."

The grandfather took a bite into his apple and chewed on it while he tried to remember the rest of the story.

"One day, the queen of the white dragons from the kingdom of Mystania came to visit. She was beautiful and powerful. She visited the dragons in the forest on the west side first and then visited the dragons on the east side. She made deals on both sides for things her kingdom didn't have. She went away very happy.

"But the east and west dragons were not happy. The east thought the west dragons had struck a better deal: lots of wood and grains. The west thought the east dragons had struck a better deal: lots of clay and sand for the dragons in Mystania to build lairs. The east and west dragons became jealous of each other. There was a huge fight in the skies.

"The battle was vicious and drawn out. Many dragons on both sides died. Eventually, all the dragons died but one. One male dragon was badly injured. He limped his way to the caves in the cliffs. He didn't quite make it inside." The grandfather pointed to the entrance of the nearest cave. "The injured dragon stayed there doing his best to rest his battered body." The grandfather pointed again. He drew in the air a shape of the spines and pointed out the head to a dragon shaped rock near the entrance.

"That is his body. When the white dragon from Mystania arrived to collect her first lot of goods she noticed many dragons were dead. When she was flying over the island, she realised a big battle had taken place. She saw many dead dragons but the one beside the cave was the only dragon which was alive. She saw he was in great pain and took pity on him. To stop the pain, she cast a spell which turned him into stone. He suffered no more.

"The white dragon just took everything she wanted from both sides. She came back two more times and visited the cave where the dragon had turned to stone. As legend is said, she laid three eggs in the cave. One egg was bronze, one was silver and one was gold. She patted the stone dragon and said his job was to guard her eggs until she came back. She never did come back. As much as anyone knows, the eggs are still in the cave being guarded by this stone dragon."

The grandfather took another bite of his apple. "That is how the island got its name. Many dead dragon bodies in battle dropped into the lake, and when their bodies touched the water, they turned to stone. If you go under the water, you can still see the spines of the dead dragons and in some places parts of their body. The dragons were gone forever."
"Aw, Granddad, do you expect us to believe that story?" asked Adam.
"Believe what you like. As far as I know, it is true."
"Can we go into the cave?" asked Evette.

"Just close to the entrance. It is too dangerous to go inside," warned the grandfather.

They walked over to the cave entrance. It was very dark. Adam took a few steps inside and then came back out. "It gets really dark very quickly in there. We need a torch." The grandfather said in a stern voice, "The entrance is as far as we go. It is too dangerous. In the past, people have gone in and never came out. Sometimes their belongings wash ashore, never their bodies. No rescue party wants to go in as they also fear not returning. In the past, people placed a wire netting just three meters inside to stop other people going in and disappearing. No one understands why, how the netting came off and washed ashore. There is something creepy in there."

Adam asked, "Creepy? If bodies don't come out, then the white dragon or her children must be inside. They must have eaten the bodies."

"Ew!" said Evette as she screwed up her face. "That's disgusting."

The grandfather stood up. "Time to leave and head back home. Your mother will be picking you up soon."

"Granddad," asked Adam, "can we come back here again?"

"Maybe tomorrow. There is another cave we can look at. It's further around."

On the next visit to the grandparents' home, both grandparents took the twins to the next cave. This cave was further back from the shore. The entrance was half hidden by fallen rocks. They walked around the fallen rocks to the entrance. This time the grandfather had a torch.

He shone the torch around the cave. "This cave is safe to go into. It is not much more than a hole in the mountain side. But you still have to be careful as rocks fall all the time. They are slowly closing the cave's entrance."

The group walked in until they reached the back wall. They turned around to see the bright sky and the lake's edge. The grandmother spoke, "If you stand over here." She walked to a rock on the sandy floor and stood on top of it, "you can see the distant mountains which have snow peaks. That is where the white dragon was supposed to come from."

The twins crowded onto the rock and looked towards the mountains. Unimpressed by the view, they stood down and said nothing.

"Are you sure about that?" asked Adam. The grandfather stood on the rock and pointed. "You can see the back of the white dragon. She turned into a mountain and the tops are her spiny back."

Evette tugged on Adam's sleeve and rolled her eyes. She whispered, "They are teasing us. White dragons, dragons turning to rocks, dragon wars. Ugh. I can see why they never told us how this island got its name. Too wacky."

Adam whispered back, "A fun wacky. Play along. Old people need to think they are being taken seriously. Shh."

Adam rejoined his grandfather on the rock. "Oh, I can see the spines. Wow. Can we go over there?"

"No," replied the grandmother. "That is the boundary of this country. We need special passes to go over and to the other side. It is very difficult to get passes." She looked at the twins. "It is easier to go west and into the forest. No passes required but you do need a guide as you can get lost in the forest."

Adam screwed up his face. "Forests are boring. Just trees and more trees."

Evette chimed in, "Bugs and some birds. Boring!"

"I know why we don't need passes for the forest," said Adam. "Nobody wants to live in that place."

"Shh," said his grandmother. "The forest has many secrets. You just have to find them."

Evette scoffed, "Secrets. No one disappears. They all get found. But the cave we passed, the one we saw yesterday, has a big secret. Missing people."

Adam agreed with her, "The cave has secrets. Creepy secrets. That is more interesting."

Chapter 3

School had started again. The twins were doing their usual naughty tricks.

A man came to visit the school. He wore black trousers and jacket with a white shirt. Around his neck was a bow tie. The teachers had asked him to come and speak about the trails and the new cabins built in the forest on the west side. At the end he asked the children to draw what they just might see in the forest at night.

Adam and Evette stared at their blank paper. Eventually, Evette picked up her black pencil and coloured the whole page black leaving tiny bits white and a circle for a moon. She added some shapes in grey for leaves. Where she missed, she called stars. Adam on the other hand drew a penguin with slightly distorted beak. It looked a bit creepy. When the man saw the two pictures he said softly to Evette, "Okay that is a start. Now add some birds."
Evette thought for a second and said, "Adam drew a bird you might see."

The man looked at Adam's drawing, and smirked. "Adam, penguins don't live in the forest."

Adam looked at the man and then back at his picture. "I am terrible at drawing birds. It's a picture of you. You said you stayed overnight in a tent when you were building cabins. You said you go to the cabins to check on people to make sure they are safe at night. Creepy. The uniform you are wearing looks like a penguin and has a penguin logo. If there are no penguins there, why do you have a penguin on your shirt?"

The man pulled back for a second. "The money raised goes to penguin conservation."

Adam wanted to say more but he saw his teacher give a stern look.

Adam quickly drew an owl as the man watched. There are no owls in this forest."

Adam quickly drew a dragon falling from the sky. "Now," he said getting irritated having to draw another picture. "My last picture. No more."

The man looked at the picture. "Dragons don't exist."

Adam got frustrated and yelled, "I am looking at one now!"

He took himself out of the classroom.

When the teacher caught up with him outside, she said, "That was not nice calling the man a names: a penguin, an owl and a dragon."

Adam grew angrier, "He dresses like a penguin, watches everyone like an owl and acts like a dragon." Adam then said, "I have had enough. I'm going home. Honesty is not appreciated in this place. Before the holidays, you said I had to be honest and say what I see and not make things up. I did just that and I still get into trouble."

It was the weekend again. Adam and Evette walked to the Northville shops. The other children stepped away when they saw them. Adam pretended to be a penguin and waddled towards them. Evette flapped her arms and crowed like a rooster. They moved back.

They walked towards the beach on Northville. They looked at the rocks and the cliffs nearby. "Let's go exploring" said Adam. "Let's see if there are any caves around here." Evette followed. As the twins walked, they pulled faces and made noises of birds. They laughed at the faces the people made when they pulled back away from them.

Evette pointed to a cluster of rocks. "Let's go over there."

Adam followed. They walked around the rocks and close to the cliff face. No caves. They moved further down the beach. There was a tiny cave just tall enough for them to stand upright. It went deep into the cliff wall. Adam who was carrying a torch with his drink in his backpack, pulled out the torch. They followed the tunnel. Then there was daylight again. They were behind a bank. Adam and Evette gasped at the discovery. "No one would believe us the bank had a tunnel to the beach." They decided to keep it quiet.

The next weekend, the grandparents were looking after them while their parents went to the mainland on the eastern side to buy some building material. Their parents were going to build a cubby house for them at the grandparents' home.

Adam and Evette went to the Eastpit beach. They walked along the beach to the small cave. They decided to explore this cave in detail. They found some pieces of bones and tried working out what animal it was. Then using their hands, they dug a hole in the sandy floor. They were now pretending to be pirates looking for treasure.

Evette felt something. She pushed the sand away. It was a ring, a very old ring. She called out, "I found treasure!" she slipped the much too big ring on her tiny ring finger. Adam smiled. "Where did you find it?"

Evette pointed to the hole. "There." She took the ring off and placed it on the rock where she, Adam and her grandparents stood a few weeks before and was now the place where they had placed their backpacks. She helped Adam dig up the sand. More pieces of jewellery were found: two more rings, a few gold chains and some loose gemstones. They looked at the pile of treasure on the rock. Adam said, "We are rich, very rich. Where do we keep it? We can't take it home."

Evette looked at her backpack. "Put it in here. Let's bury the backpack with all the jewellery in it. I know Mum and Dad will be mad at me for 'losing' my backpack." She began to empty her backpack of food and water. Adam slowly placed them in his backpack as he thought of a place to hide the jewellery.
"How about we bury the backpack between this rock and the cave wall. It will be easier to find it again," suggested Adam.

Adam and Evette dug with their hands in the new spot. They dug a deep hole, much deeper than the one they found the jewellery. They covered the spot and stomped their feet on the ground. Then they stomped the ground all around the rock. "We better get back. It's getting late."

On Sunday, they were at the grandparents' home again helping their father build the cubby house.

It was quite large with two rooms and a stool in each. Their grandmother gave them some old sheets for them to do as they pleased. Evette said softly to Adam, "We can dig up the treasure and hide it in here."

"No. Too risky," said Adam as he watched his father take a large sheet of ply to make a crude ceiling.

Then Adam had an idea. "Dad. Can we change the ceiling?"

His father looked at Adam with curiosity. "What do you want?"

"Half a ceiling. A gap halfway." He pointed to the halfway mark. He stood up under the area.

"My head just about touches the ceiling now. If there is a half ceiling, I can stand upright here when I am taller."

His father nodded. "That's a good idea. That will be like a shelf."

Evettte was looking on. "Add a door and then we can put things away…err keep the place tidy."

Adam grinned. "That's really a good idea. A lock too."

The father looked at the twins. "You two are up to something. Why would you want a lock?"

Adam looked around searching for an answer. "Just suppose what we have here, we think is valuable to us. It may be junk to someone else, but to us, it is valuable. I would like to know that thing is safe. We are not here every day. A locked door would make us sleep better if we knew it was safe."

Their father chuckled, "Okay. A lock on a door."

He turned to Evette. "Do you want a cupboard too?"

Evette thought for a while. "Mmm. Yep." She drew a picture on a scrap piece of paper.

She drew Adam's side first. "Put a wall here so my stuff doesn't slide across to Adam's side."

She drew her side. "I would like a box to fit inside the space. The box is divided down the middle to keep things tidy, a bit like the shelf in the kitchen. The box only goes halfway back to make a secret hiding place. When I am away, I can turn the box around and it looks like part of the half ceiling. Yep."

Her father gave her a frown but didn't say anything. He thought, *Something is going on. I wonder what these two are up too.* "Okay, m'lady, a box it will be."

When the cubby house was finished, Evette and Adam painted it. They started with the roof. They made it dark green. They painted the walls two different colours. Adam painted his pale green and Evette painted hers a darker green. Both painted the doors white and wrote their name on a door in black. They stood back and looked at the paint job.

Adam said, "The doors are the wrong colour."
What do you mean?" asked Evette.
"The place is all green like an army tent. Change the doors by blotching the greens over them. We can leave our names on." Adam took his dark green paint and made blobs over the door. Then he added the roof colour. Then he took Evette's paint and placed blobs around. He stood back for a second before adding blobs of black. "There," he said as he stood back. "Just like an army tent."

Evette looked at the work and walked around the cubby house. She started to paint her door the same way but not as much blobs. She went to her side of the cubby and started doing the same. Adam decided to copy. "Shall we do the back as well?" he asked her. Both looked at the back.

"Yeah," said Evette. "But we have a problem… not enough green paint." They looked at the cans.

Adam said a bit disappointed, "There is some black left and…just black. I don't think it will be necessary to paint the wall again. It is at the back and close to the fence."

"Okay. We are finished," said Evette. She added, "We are going to cop it. Our clothes are paint stained. We have paint on us."

Their mother looked at them as they approached the back stairs of the grandparents' house.

"You two were very busy. Did you have fun?" she asked.

The twins smiled. "Yep. Sorry about the mess," said Evette.

"Before you to clean up, put the empty cans in the bin." She waited until the task was done.

"Evette and Adam, place your old t-shirt and old blouse in the same bin. Then come inside."

Their mother waited. "Evette first. Get in the shower."

After school on Monday afternoon, Adam asked Evette, "Let's dig up the treasure and hide it in the cubby." "Okay. We have to be quick. Mum won't like us being so late."

When they approached the small Eastpit cave, they stopped. Other people were going into the cave where the treasure was hidden. One man was holding a camp shovel. "Let's go out of here," said Adam. "Run!"

The twins ran as fast as they could along the beach. Evette looked over her shoulder to see the people yelling at each other. She turned to run faster. Adam was ahead of her. There was a bang. The twins looked back. Someone was holding a gun. A person was injured and on the ground. The twins ran faster.

When they reached home, they puffed. "Mum, we saw someone on the Eastpit beach going in the small cave. We were going to play there but men were going in. One carried a shovel. Then we heard them yelling at each other. Then we heard a bang. We turned around and saw a man holding a gun and the other was on the ground. We ran all the way home."

Their mother looked at them with shock. "What were you doing on the beach? You are supposed to come home after school."

Adam's puffing was slowing down. "We know. We just wanted to play there. We took off really fast. I don't think the man with the gun saw us." Their mother knew from experience, the twins would tell a few lies, *But this one, she thought, was not a lie.* They didn't have the imagination for that. She called the police.

The police came and took notes. The twins, with their mother and the police went to the beach where the shooting took place. The police searched the sand for signs of blood or anything else. They went into the cave and saw a hole in the ground. They knew something had happened here. Something was buried and retrieved. Whatever it was, it was gone. Whatever it was, it was enough to make one person shoot another. The police took a photo of the hole in the cave floor.

One policeman said to Adam, Evette and to their mother, Mary, "Someone was here and since gone. They made a hole in the middle of the floor. There is no blood on the beach." He was about to say more when his mini shoulder radio crackled, "All police go to the bank. There has been a robbery."

The police began running back to their car. When the twins heard the announcement of the robbery and saw the police running back to their car, Adam saw it was pointless trying to call after them. He wanted to mention the cave to the bank. Adam said to Evette, "I bet they escape through the cave."

"What are you talking about?" asked their mother.
"There is a cave near the Northville beach entrance. The cave goes up to the bank. Anyone can come and go without being seen. We can show you."
Mary pulled them back. "Not now. The police are busy."
Adam shrugged. "They will get away. I bet they have a dingy ready for their escape to the mainland."
"How do you know that?" asked their mother.
"If a tunnel goes to a beach, they would go to the bank by the cave where no one could see them coming or going. While the police are running around like lost chooks, the robbers are speeding away in a dingy." There was a sound of a dingy travelling high speed towards the mainland.

They all looked towards the sound. Evette said in a loud voice, "That is one of the men we saw. The one in the front shot another man! Adam was right. They are escaping by dingy!"

Adam sighed. "They got away."

Chapter 4

It was Wednesday afternoon after school when the twins arrived home, they saw a police car in the driveway. They wondered what was happening. Their mother met them at the door and quickly placed their bags in a cupboard. She said softly, "The police are here. They want to know more about the cave to the bank."

The twins were ushered into the lounge room. They sat opposite the police. The policeman who was at the Eastpit beach was there. He gave a friendly smile. "Hello. Did you have a good day at school?"
The twins shook their heads. Adam spoke, "We don't like school that much."
"Oh," said another policeman who hadn't said a word until then.
The first policeman spoke, "Your mother told me you all saw a dingy speed away after we were called to the bank." The twins nodded. "Your mother said you saw the man with a gun the other day and he was driving the boat." Both nodded.

"Can you two come with your mother and show us the tunnel in the cave?"

The twins nodded. "We looked behind the bank and didn't see any other places they could escape to," said the policeman.

Adam spoke, "We were surprised it came out behind the bank. It is a bit hidden behind some bushes."

The twins showed the two policeman the cave entrance and further inside to the tunnel. Adam and Evette led the way. The policemen with a few others brought some high-powered lamps. As they walked, one policeman said, "This was hand made. Look at the marks on the wall. They used a jackhammer for the most difficult parts and maybe shovels for the soft bits." Adam looked at the wall to see what the policeman was talking about. He knew his small torch would never have picked that up. It was just enough for them to see their way through the cave.

They came to rear of the bank. Evette and Adam pushed a bush to one side to guide the men out.

They all stared at the back of the bank. "What are you going to do now?" asked Adam.

The policeman didn't answer. "Thank you for helping us. You can both go home with your mother. Thanks again for your help. Tomorrow after school, I want you all to come to the station. Evette, do you think you can remember what the man with the gun looks like? We need you to draw a picture of him." Evette looked stony faced and pulled out a picture of a face she drew in her lunch break. "One like this?" she asked. She showed a picture of a man with a snarl on his face. The policeman took the picture and looked at it carefully, "Do you mind if we take this?"

"As long as you give it back when you are finished. It took me all my lunch break to draw it."

The policeman nodded. "I think we can do that. But still come to the station. We can use this to start the composite picture."

Adam misheard the word. "Compost picture? What's that?"

"Not compost," the policeman chuckled. "Composite. When you get there, we will show you."

Chapter 5

Two months went by before the twins were able to be on the beach at Eastpit.

They were staying with their grandparents. They played in the cubby house for the first time in months. Then one afternoon, when the grandparents were sleeping, they sneaked away to the cave where they had buried the treasure months before. They dug up Evette's old backpack and looked in. Everything was still inside. They buried the treasure again, stomped on the sand and walked back home.

The next day they went to the beach again. "Let's look inside where the people disappear," suggested Evette.
Adam hesitated. "Only as far as the daylight goes. That cave is a bit creepy. It could be full of ghosts."
"Aw! Come off it. Pull my other leg. Okay. Just where the light is. I'm taking a torch."

The twins slipped away again. They came to the cave entrance where the rocks on one side looked like a sleeping dragon. They stood outside, hesitating at first. They stood close to each other as Evette turned on her torch. She shone the torch around the entrance. "Hey look! There is shelf up there. One made of dirt. Let's climb up and have a look…. Just at the entrance. The shelf is just above the cave entrance, so we aren't going deep inside, not even a metre."

The twins slowly climbed up to the earth shelf. Evette shone her torch down the length of the shelf. She spotted something shiny.
"Something is there at the back. It can't be far down because my torch only goes five meters."

Evette shone the torch down the back of the tunnel at the same time a gust of wind rushed through the cave. The whistling sound made the twins turn around and jump down from the shelf.

Evette puffed as they ran outside again. "That must have been the white dragon's babies. They have hatched."
Adam spoke slowly, "The missing people must have been eaten by the baby dragons. I'm not going in there again. I don't want to be their dinner." Just then another strong gust of wind whistle past. It made the same noise. The twins laughed. "We are stupid," said Evette. "It was only the wind.

Gee, I feel really stupid. Let's go and have another look before we go home."

"Let's go," said Adam as he started to walk inside the cave and headed directly for the shelf.

Evette shone her torch down to the back. She walked slowly with Adam close behind. She moved the torch to shine on the ground and to the sides before taking any steps. When they reached the back of the mini cave, they shone it on the shiny object. "What is it?" she asked Adam.

"I don't know. Let's see if we can dig it out," he suggested.

He started to claw the dirt with his fingers. "It's too hard. We need something sharp like a stick or a knife or a small shovel." He stopped digging. "Let's come back when we can, and bring something to dig this out."

Evette said, "I have some pocket money saved up. Let's buy our own tools. Granddad is going to the hardware shop tomorrow. I heard him say that to grandma. He wants to fix the kitchen tiles. He said something about grouting. Whatever that is. I will use my money to buy a small tool."

"Okay," said Adam. "I will bring mine as well. Just in case you don't have enough." On the way back to their grandparents' home, the twins talked about what the object could be.

It was another week before the twins could sneak away. Evette was armed with a torch, food, water and a hand garden fork which she already used to help her grandmother to weed the garden. Adam bought a small trowel which he too had used in the garden. He also had his own water and food tucked in his backpack.

At the cave they climbed to the earth shelf. They pulled out their tools and started to work. Slowly, the dirt gave way. Adam gave the object a tug. It came free. It was a brass key. "We did all that work for a key?"
"Let me have a look at it," said Evette. She held it up to eye level and shone the torch on it. She sighed. "I think we better go outside and look at this carefully. I think I see some writing on it."
She grinned. "A magic key?"
"Yeah. Right," scoffed Adam.

Back at their grandparents' home, Evette drew a picture of the key. Adam looked on. "That funny writing on it, can you write it on this paper? Just the writing. Then we can take it to the library to see if there is anything to help us translate it."

Instead of being in the playground at school, the twins went to the school library. They first searched the very few reference books and then went to the internet. Nothing came up. They asked the librarian for help to decipher the script. The librarian looked at the paper Adam gave her. "Where did you find this?"
"We found it on a bit of driftwood," lied Adam. "Is it a code or something?"

The librarian thought for a second before moving to another part of the library. She flipped through pages with lots of scripts from around the world. It didn't match any of them. She sighed. "I really can't help you. It looks a bit like ancient Celt, but that is not right either. Maybe the people at the museum can help." She gave back the script.

On the weekend they convinced their father they wanted a trip to the local museum. He thought it a bit strange as they always refused to go there before.

In the time they were there, they walked around looking at the different displays before going into the theatre where there was an animated picture on how Dragon's Lair got its name. In the movie they showed some writing found on a door architrave. Adam gasped and nudged Evette. "That's the same waiting on the paper." He pulled out the paper he carried in his pocket. He rushed out of the room. Evette followed. Their father followed behind, not knowing what made the twins run out like the place was on fire. He found them talking to a staff member who was pointing to a small recess at the back of a room they had already been in.

They ran to the room and knocked on the door. An elderly man slowly opened the door. Not giving the man a chance to say hello, they started talking quickly about the piece of paper they were holding up far too close to his eyes. The man slowly lowered their hand with the note just as their father came up behind. He spoke sternly. "You just don't run out of the theatre like that ever again. And you don't disturb staff from their work. Apologise."
Adam looked at his father with defiance. Evette screwed up her face in anger. Adam said, "We just want this translated. That is all."

The old man took the piece of paper. He looked at it. "My, my. Where did you find this?"

Adam said, "We copied it from an object. It was very rusted. I don't think we copied it right as bits were missing. It crumpled up as we tried to copy the writing."

"Adam. Evette. Don't bother this man. He has important work to do," said their father.

"No. no. This is a welcomed and unexpected break from the usual boring things. Come inside."

The old man pulled up chairs for the three unexpected guests. He turned to his desk and pulled out an old book. He flipped through the pages stopping now and then before moving to another page. He turned to the children, "Exactly where did you find the rusted object?'

Adam pulled out a bag of rust with a few very rusted odd shaped objects inside. He gave the bag to the man. "The more we touched it, the more it crumbled up. Sorry."

The man looked at the useless bag and suspected he was being lied to. He played along with that part of the game but was quite serious about the copied script.

"The script says it belonged to the white dragon. It comes with a warning. Now, I am not sure if I am translating it

right, and as you say, bits are not there. That makes it a wee bit harder." The old man coughed and looked at the children. "It says it is the key to a chest of drawers where the white dragon laid her eggs. It says if the finder of the key finds the chest and opens it, their life will change forever. It can be good or bad. Good is very, very good. Bad is disastrous."
"What's in the chest?" asked Evette.

The old man shrugged. "I honestly don't know. I have never heard of this chest of drawers story before. It is best the chest stays hidden. It is much safer for all. Do you mind if I made a photocopy?"
Evette said, "No." She shrugged at the request. She and Adam had they original and the key. No one else was going to know about that. The old man handed back the paper.

"Thank you," said the twins together. Their father shook the old man's hand.
The old man smiled. "They look like a handful."
"That is not half of it," replied the father. "Thank you again for your time."

When they left the elderly man picked up the phone. He spoke to someone about the script which he was looking at as he spoke. He looked at the bag of rust and said, "The children gave me, what I believe to be, worthless a bag of dust. I would like it analysed. I will come to the lab with the bag."

It was another month before the twins had a chance to go back to the cave where they found the key. "Where do we start looking?" asked Evette.

"Your guess is as good as mine. We can start digging around the place where we found the key."

"No. No," said Evette. "Your cubby house has a key to the cupboard. You don't leave the key in the lock. There is no point in a lock with a key inside it. Where do put the key in your cubby?"

Adam hesitated as he didn't want to reveal where he hid it. Then he thought, *I could find another place to hide it.* "On the opposite side of the cubby. Behind stuff."

They looked directly across the other side of the entrance. They saw nothing. Adam climbed up to the shelf again. He sat there looking across the cave and around. "Hand me your torch." He shone the torch up and down the other side. "Damn it. There is another shelf way up there." He pointed to a darkened space on the other side. He jumped down from the earth shelf.

"How high up?" Evette asked.

"Too high. We will need a ladder or find another way up." He pointed to a place where Evette struggled to see.

"We will have to come back another day," said Adam. "We need to do some planning."

Chapter 6

Three days passed before the twins sneaked out again to the cave. This time they had more tools.

"This is going to take forever to get to that ledge," said Evette.

"Yeah. I know. I hope it is worth it. How many torches did you bring?"

"This time, two and extra batteries."

"I borrowed dad's big torch and have two small ones of my own. I think we have enough," said Adam.

They chipped away at the vertical wall. After twenty minutes they made a one foothold in the dirt and rock mix. The waste material was stacked like a step. That would be the only step they would make. The next foothold took longer. There were more rocks than dirt.

They did three footholds before deciding to pack up. They hoped they could come back the next day. They cleaned themselves up by taking a quick dip in the lake with their clothes on. They knew they would almost be dry by the time they reached their grandparents' home.

It was another week before the twins were able to be back at the cave. This time, they dug three more footholds up the same wall. "Now it was looking like a built-in ladder," said Evette feeling proud of their joint effort.

"Just four more steps to make," said Adam. "It's time to pack up and get back."

They packed their tools and torches into their back packs.

Another week went by. The twins were back at the cave. This time, they worked extra hard and faster to build four more steps. When they were at the top of the ledge, they stood at the entrance to the new section of the cave. They turned on all the torches for a quick look before going back. They couldn't see anything that was interesting. They knew they had to come back another day.

It was close to winter. The days were getting shorter and cooler. The twins knew not many people would be outside and fewer would be down the beach area, let alone the main cave. They knew their steps were close to the cave entrance and just hoped no one went inside if they visited the cave. Anyone going inside would easily see the steps. They hoped against all odds no one went there and climbed their ladder.

In this time the twins played in their cubby house whenever they visited their grandparents. They also spent time planning their next move and doing extra tasks to earn some pocket money. They guessed they may need to buy more equipment. They planned their extra chores in the home and outside. By the end of winter, they made close to fifty dollars each.

About mid-spring, they went back to the cave. The steps were still there. They climbed the steps. The cave was shorter than the cave across the other side. The roof dipped down. Adam and Evette had to bend over halfway to reach the back wall. They sat down. "That was not exiting," said Evette. She shone the torch around the cave. Adam thought he saw another cave.

"Shine your torch back there." He pulled out his larger torch. He crawled back halfway before standing up.

"It's another shelf. Look! We need to make another ladder. Two steps should do it."

They got to work. Two more steps were made. This time Evette went first. She said, "This looks better. Come on up." Adam climbed up and looked around. He smiled. He saw what Evette was looking at. There was something buried in the wall. Only an old-fashioned brass knob could be seen. "Let's dig around that and see what it is," said Adam who was now very excited.

The twins chipped at the dry dirt for an hour. Then stopped to look at the forming shape.

"What do you think it is?" asked Evette.

"Well it looks like the same stuff the key was made of. I asked Granddad what that kind of metal was when I showed him a padlock made of the same stuff. He called it brass. Yeah. Brass. Keep clearing the front part."

Another thirty minutes passed. The front of the chest was exposed. The edges at the side came into view. They saw the edge to the top. They stopped clearing the dirt away knowing, this was enough to start investigating the chest. Evette looked at the chest front. "Unusual. I thought chests had a lid that flips open at the top. This has drawers top to bottom." The drawers had two large brass knobs. It was one of these knobs which had attracted their attention at the start. The twins saw a keyhole in the centre drawer but took no notice of it.

Evette tried to pull open on the large top drawer. It didn't move. Adam had a go. He tugged harder and harder. He yelled and swore. "All this hard work and the thing is jammed! Grr"

"Try the next drawer," suggested Evette. Adam and Evette took turns. Nothing happened.
"Try the next drawer." Adam puffed.

The very bottom drawer was pulled and tugged at the knobs. Nothing moved. Adam yelled in frustration. He kicked the bottom drawer. Something made a noise. He looked at the bottom again. He gave it another pull. It slid out. Nothing was inside. He hit the other drawers. All slowly opened when he and Evette tugged at them. Nothing. "What a waste of time!" said Evette equally upset.

She started to push the drawers back into position. She started with the top drawer and slowly moved down to the bottom. Then she heard a click. She pulled open the bottom drawer again.
"Hey. Look at this. It was a magic drawer." She slid the door back in. Nothing. She pulled it out completely and slid the drawer back in. Click. She opened the drawer again. Inside

was a small box. Evette and Adam looked at the box. "Let's take it back to the cubby house. We will work out how to open it there. It's getting late. We better get going." Evette stuffed the box into her backpack.

They went to their grandparents' home as fast as they could and straight into the cubby house.

Their grandmother saw them rush by her and straight to the cubby house. Normally, they would say hello to her, but this time, they ran past her as if she wasn't there. Normally, each would go to their separate spaces but, this time they went into Adam's side. *Odd*, she thought. She waited for them to come out. They didn't. She went back to the kitchen to prepare dinner. It was getting dark. The twins were still inside the cubby house. *They are up to something*, she thought. *They must have something they want to keep secret.* She watched them from the kitchen window. They eventually came out. "Hi, grandma. What's for dinner?"

The grandmother looked at them. "Hello would have been nice nearly two hours ago. Clean up. You two look like you have been playing in the dirt pit. What were you two doing in there so long? Normally, you two go into your own side and play running in and out or taking food in there. What have you got that's so interesting?"

"Nothing," chorused the twins. Their grandmother returned the bowl of food to the kitchen bench.

"Then it is nothing for dinner until you tell me. Clean up. Then come back. No tall stories."

Ten minutes later, the twins were sitting at the table with clean hands and fresh clothes.

"We found an old box. We couldn't work out how to open it. It is like a puzzle box in the toyshop window in Southville. It must have been tossed out as it is very grubby."

"Where did you find this old box?"

"At the beach," said Evette before Adam could say another word or say a place that was different to her idea.

"Can I have a look at it?" asked the grandmother.

Both shook their heads. "We like doing puzzles. It will give us something to do….and out of mischief. Tomorrow we are going to be in the cubby house and try to work it out," said Adam.

"We won't fight. We will be taking turns. Five minutes by the clock. The old clock you gave me only needed batteries to make it work."

"Eat up your meal. Your father will be here soon to pick you up."

On the next visit to the grandparents' home, the twins ran directly to the cubby house yelling hello to both grandparents over their shoulders.

Tom said, "I didn't think the cubby house was going to be so popular."

"They found an old puzzle box down the beach. They want to open it up by themselves. Last time they were in there for two hours. I almost had to drag them out." said Tom's mother, Sally.

"I went in the cubby. You did a marvellous job. They hid the box somewhere. I opened up all the hidey-holes. The box wasn't in there. They must have hidden it somewhere else," said Tom's father, Steve.

"Those two are up to something. I better get going. I'll pick them up late this afternoon," said Tom as he gave his parents a peck on the cheek.

*****

Adam examined the box. He pushed pulled, twisted everything he could think of. Evette said, "Maybe it is jammed like the big chest of drawers was. Try dropping it."

Adam stood up as tall as he could in the cubby house and raised an arm. He dropped the box. Thump!

"Try again," said Evette as she handed the box to Adam. Try another angle." Adam flipped the box on to its lid and let it drop. Thunk! Pop. The lid came off.

They looked in the box. Nothing was inside. Evette sighed. "Maybe it has another secret compartment." She let Adam investigate the box while she looked at the lid which had come off on the second impact.

"Ah Ha!" said Adam when he noticed the bottom of the box inside was shallower than what it looked outside. He tossed the box around to examine the outside. *I wonder*, he thought as he tried to dig his fingernails into what looked like a crack. "Bingo!" He slowly pulled the false base out.

"You're kidding me. Nothing again!" Evette looked at the mini drawer which was moved out of its slot. "Slide it back in," she suggested.

Adam slid the drawer in and pulled it out. This time the drawer was opened up. "Oh no. A coin. It's an old coin." Both children looked at the coin. Evette said, "It has the old-style writing on it. I don't think we should take it to the museum for translation. They will want to keep it. And all we get is an ice cream or some other type of sweets. We will be ripped off and questioned. I don't want to be questioned about where we found it."

Adam looked at the coin again. "You're right. I'll lock the box on my side of the cubby and you hide the coin behind your shelf. Put it in this jar. Do you want to go back to that old chest of drawers? This time we take the key and see if it fits the locks."

Evette nodded. "I will let grandma know we are going to the beach again."

One: *Assist an elderly person who is not related to you.*
It can be any task an elderly person is having trouble completing.

Chapter 7

The twins went to the cave. They climbed the first carved out ladder and then up the small one.

Adam took the key out of his bag and tried to slip it into the only keyhole which was in the middle drawer. It wouldn't fit. He groaned.

"The keyhole is blocked up with dirt. We have to clean it out," he said somewhat frustrated. He put the key in the backpack and pulled out a piece of wire.

"Where did you get that?" asked Evette.

"I found it on the road. Let's have a go digging the dirt out with this."

When they thought they had scrapped the dirt out, Adam slipped the key in again. He tried turning it. It moved a bit but not enough to open the drawer. Evette said, "Stand aside." She gave it a hard thump at the front. "See if there is more dirt inside." Adam picked the keyhole. More dirt fell out. He tried the key again. *Click*! "Nothing," yelled Adam.

Then there was a noise. The chest of drawers shook. Adam and Evette ran to the edge of the ledge. A bright glow of light shone from behind. The chest of drawers swung back. It was a door.

The twins walked slowly to the opening and looked inside. They gasped. It was another world. They hesitated. Evette took a step just inside the door. "Oh my God! It's beautiful in here. Come on and look." Adam took a step inside the door. He smiled as he looked around. "Beautiful. Just beautiful." He took another step but rushed back to the door pulling Evette with him. "Did you see the giant birds? One looked like a jumbo turkey which could feed all of Dragon's Lair. Then there was one which looked like a cross between a flamingo with its head and legs and an eagle with huge black wings. It was bigger than that turkey. The one that scared me most was the one with bat wings and a pelican head. That was the biggest and ugliest of them all."

Evette shook her head. She returned to where she was earlier before Adam pulled her back. This time she walked a tiny bit further when she saw some eggs. She stopped and picked up three eggs. One was bronze, one was silver, and one was gold. She shoved them quickly and carefully into her backpack.

"Let's get out of here before one of the birds discovers they are missing. Shut the door too." The twins went home with the eggs.

Adam put the eggs in the box he hid earlier. "Let's see if they will hatch. Maybe they won't because it is not in its nest." "I think you are right. If they haven't hatched by the next visit, we will return them," said Evette, who was now feeling a touch guilty for stealing the eggs.

It was close to a week before the twins returned to their grandparents' home. They rushed to the cubby and pulled out the box with the eggs. Adam quickly opened the box. "One egg has a crack! The bronze egg has cracked!" The egg spat out a piece of paper. Adam showed Evette the paper. Evette held the paper when she tried to read it. "Why does it have to be in that old-fashioned writing?" said Evette disappointed with the find.

Suddenly, the paper started to glow. Evette dropped the paper thinking it might burn her fingers. The ancient words disappeared to be replaced by modern writing. Adam carefully picked up the paper to read it.

"By ancient law of the dragons, the finder or finders of this bronze egg must complete three tasks. Failure to compete the tasks will result in uncomfortable punishments. Complete the tasks before the deadline, good things will happen.

Task One. Assist an elderly person who is not related to you. It can be any task the elderly person is having trouble completing. If you finish the task you will have good fortune. If not, you may not like what happens to you. The only way to reverse the punishment is to try the task again.

Task Two. Make some food and give it to a homeless person. If you don't do the task, something bad will happen and it won't stop until you do the task again.

Task Three. Go to the forest on the west side and bring back four black stones and a handful of black dirt. If you don't do the task, something bad will happen. Do the task and something good will happen. You can do the tasks in any order, but you have one month to complete everything. If you don't complete all three, then you may not like what will happen to you."

Adam who was also reading the message put the paper down. "Is this for real?" The paper flew up and went inside the egg. This time the bronze egg spoke in a squeaky voice, "Yes. It is real."

The twins stared at the egg. Evette stuttered. "Th ..Th..The egg talks."

The egg squeaked again, "Of course, I talk. Now start working on your tasks. You have one month."

Adam and Evette sat quietly, not believing what had happened. After a while, Adam spoke.

"Do you think it will punish us for not doing the tasks?" He placed the egg back in the box with the other eggs. Adam hid the box in his new hiding place, under a lose floorboard. "It has scared me into doing it some things. Helping old people? Cooking some food for a homeless person? Have you seen any homeless people on Dragon's Lair?"

Adam shook his head. "Nope. Maybe on the mainland. Not here."

"I don't like going to that forest. Finding black stones and some dirt. Ugh! It is a national park. You're not supposed to steal from a national park. Mission impossible."

Chapter 8

Adam was clearing the dishes on the table when he asked, "Mum, have you seen any homeless people on Dragon's Lair?"

"There are a few. They sleep in the council carpark at night. There, they get a dry place to sleep at night. They also use the shower if they want to. Why do you ask?"

"Where do they go in the daytime?" asked Adam.

"Umm. I'm not sure. Some may try to find bits of work for a day or half day. Some keep out of the way of others. Sadly, some people are scared of them and chase them away. Why?"

"I was wondering. Our birthday is coming up. Instead of having a few other kids over or a sleep over, we want to do something different. Evette and I spoke about it."

"Just what do you want to do?"

"Make some dinner up and some cupcakes and give it to some homeless people. But we need to know how many there are."

"Wow. That is something very different. Very unexpected. We will slip down to the carpark and see how many homeless people there are. What exactly brought this on this idea?"

"Well," Adam coughed, "we have enough stuff. Dad built us a really cool cubby. That makes us having three homes: the cubby, here and Grandma's and Grandpa's home. These people have zilch. Is it possible to do that instead of a birthday party?"

"I will talk it over with your father. I think he will be surprised by it."

The next night the family went to the carpark where the homeless slept over night. They counted six people. Mary asked the council supervisor who was handing out some fruit, sandwiches and protein bars about the possibility of a meal for the six. She quickly explained why. The worker looked at the twins. "Okay. As long as you two do just that. No playing up."

"Promise," said the twins together.

Two nights later, the twins with their parents brought in a tub of soup, bread, individual tubs of fruit salad and cupcakes. The six homeless people took their share and smiled at the different food. Then Adam and Evette served all the food to each person. They spoke softly to each other,

"I think we did this right. Bought the bread with our own money. We made the fruit salad all by ourselves. Mum watched us make the cupcakes, and we decorated them by ourselves. We helped mum chopping the vegetables and chopping the meat for the soup. We stirred the soup when it was cooking and we helped serve it out."

"I hope so. How would a piece of paper and an egg know?" asked Evette.

Adam shrugged. "They are in the box. The box is locked away. They can't see us."

Two days later the children were in the cubby house again. They heard a rattling noise coming from under the floor boards where Adam hid the box. He took out the box. The box rattled again.

He dropped the box. "Ouch!" said the box. Adam and Evette looked at the box. The twins huddled into a corner. The box opened by itself. The bronze egg split open again and the paper flew out. It started to glow. The message appeared.

"The task of feeding a homeless person was not done right. It was supposed to be one person not six. You didn't cook all the soup and time the cupcakes in the oven. You did well to serve the meal. Here is your punishment."

There was puff of wind and glitter fell over them.

Their clothes disappeared. Old clothes raggy clothes were on their bodies. Evette cried, "That is not fair. We are kids not adults! We gave up our birthday party to do that. Our parents are not rich! You're horrible. Just horrible."

The paper glowed again. *"Sorry. Kids. Aye. You gave up your birthday to feed six people and you did help. Okay then."* Another puff of wind and more glitter. The twin looked at each other. Both screamed. They were turned into goats with horns on their forehead. The paper glowed. Adam picked it up with his mouth from the floor, "'You idiot. We are children not goats!"

"Sorry. I thought you were baby goats." The paper disappeared into the egg.

There was another puff of wind. This time the glitter flew up from the floor before disappearing. The twins were back in to being children.

Evette sighed. "Thank you. What was supposed to be the reward or the good thing that happens?"

The egg spoke in its squeaky voice. "The good thing is you are back to normal again." Adam looked at Evette. "We were conned. Gee, a piece of paper and an egg conned us."

"Not quite. Can you imagine what Mum and Dad could say if they saw us in those rags or worse still as goats with horns? They would be looking for us and thinking we were kidnapped."

"Well, we know what kind of punishment we would get. That was so scary. Never again shall we look like goats. Neve ever," said Adam.

"How are we going to do the next task? Which one shall we do, old people or the forest?"

Adam said, "We ask Mum and Dad to take us to the forest for a picnic. We have to give them time to work out a day. But in the meantime, we do the old people thing." Evette nodded.

Evette was walking down the street with her only school friend, Jane. They stopped at the post office to buy some stamps. Jane's mother, Kate wanted ten stamps. While at the post office, Evette saw an elderly couple. The man sat on the bench while his wife lined up. The old man pulled out a handkerchief and blew his nose. Jane and Evette laughed at the trumpet noise the man made.

The old lady looked at the girls and frowned. She whispered, "Young kids these days show no respect. Wait until they get old."

Jane bought her stamps and asked if Evette wanted to go to the ice cream shop. Evette agreed. They were eating their ice cream when the same old people came in. Evette watched them carefully.

The old couple bought their ice cream and went to a nearby table. Jane saw Evette watching. "Why are you staring at them?"

"I am watching in case they might need help to do something," replied Evette.

"When did you become a saint?" asked Jane very surprised at Evette's reply.

"Well, look at them. The old man has wobblily legs. The old lady has stiff fingers and her arms don't move that well. Between them, they have one working body. It won't hurt if I helped them if something happened."

"Gee. Am I with the same Evette I knew two months ago? The one who played jokes on people?"

"This is the same Evette. But now I am being more careful with my jokes or pranks. I am tired of people giving me a wide space like I have a virus when I come into view." Jane put her hand on Evette's forehead.

"Okay. You are normal. Gee, you have changed. I am not sure if I like the new Evette."

"I am still me. Look, the old people are leaving. Let's follow them for a while "Jane rolled her eyes but then thought, *She maybe planning something*.

Jane and Evette followed the old couple to the bus stop. The bus came along minutes later. Evette watched the old couple try to get on the bus.

The lady tried to hold the rail to pull herself up when she stepped on the first step. She fell backwards onto her husband who tried to catch her. He fell to the ground. Evette rushed over and helped the man and lady up and then helped him into the bus. The man smiled as he sat down beside his wife. He thanked Evette as she got off the bus. The old man smiled. "There may be some hope yet with the young people." His wife nodded.

Jane and Evette were on their way home when they came across one of the homeless people Evette had served food earlier. The rag dressed lady approached. Jane froze on the spot. Evette smiled as she said, "Hello."
The lady smiled. "Thank you for the delicious meal you and your brother cooked. It was so nice."

Evette nodded. "It was fun making that food. It was nicer serving it out. But we can't do it all the time." Without a word, Evette reached into her backpack and gave the lady her apple. "Here take it. I have more at home." The lady smiled and sniffed as a small tear trickled out. "Thank you so much." The woman tucked the apple into her pocket. "God bless you," she called as the girls walked away. Evette waved back.

Jane asked, "Why did you do that, give your apple away? And what was that all about cooking and serving food?" "This year Adam and I didn't have a birthday party. We spent the money on giving a meal to the homeless people. She was just one of them. They are mostly nice people. Just down on their luck," explained Evette.

"My God! You really did that?"

"It was not only different but was a bit of hard work. It was fun too."

"Wow, you have really changed. Here is my house. See you tomorrow."

"Yeah. Jane, don't say anything to anyone else. It will wreck my reputation."

Jane pretended to zip her mouth. She waved as she went into her yard.

Evette was around the corner from her house when she felt something on her leg. She bent down to find it was a twenty dollar note. As she looked at the note, the money disappeared, and a message appeared. *"Nicely done. Can you do something like that again?"*

"Like what? Help old people or give more food away?" asked Evette who was shocked to know the egg and the paper were watching.

"Both would be good." The paper changed into a five dollar note.

"Cheapskate," whispered Evette. "Changing the twenty dollars into five. Grr!"

When she got home, Adam was in his room playing a computer game. She knocked on his door before going in. She explained what had happened. "No way. It's creepy that they are watching what we do." Evette showed the five dollar note. Just then, her mother came in. She saw the money. Her mother gave a sigh. "You found the five dollars I lost earlier. My change purse fell open on the ground. I got all the money back but five dollars. The wind just blew it away. It went around the corner and disappeared. Thank you."

"The wind blew it onto my leg. I thought I was lucky to find the money. How come I didn't see you?" said Evette.

"I didn't see you either," said her mother. Evette handed the money back.

"You were lucky to find it. Thank you so much." The mother left the room after planting a kiss on Evette's forehead and giving her a cuddle.

Evette muttered, "I thought it was too good to be true, finding that money."

Two days later, Adam went to his friend's home. John lived near the old people's home. They played computer games for a while and then played a game in the yard. John's mother, Ellen, walked in. "I am going to work. John, your father is running a bit late so you will be here for about thirty minutes by yourselves. Is that okay?"

John nodded. As the Ellen left, Adam asked, "Where does your mother work? She is wearing a uniform."

"In the old people's nursing home," replied John.

Adam hesitated, "Do nursing home let people in to visit or help?"

"All the time," replied John. "Why?"

"Well, it may seem strange, but can I look inside?"

John saw his mother starting to walk down the street. He yelled, "Mum! Mum! Can we come with you for a little while?"

John's mother looked a bit surprised. "Lock the door and come along."

At the nursing home Adam was surprised to see just how many people there were. Some were moving around quite well, while other used a walking frame. Others he saw were just sitting in a chair and staring into space. Adam, thought, *They are just staring into nothingness.* Remembering what the task he had to do, he looked around with sharpened eyes, searching for a task.

He was about to leave the lounge area when an old man held his hand. "Come and sit down with me. I want you to read the newspaper to me. My eyes are not very good. Come."

The old man patted the seat beside him and held up the newspaper. Adam hesitated, knowing he wasn't a very good reader and began to read the headlines. The old man would say, "Read that article" or "skip over that one." As Adam read, his reading improved. He felt more confident. He started to like reading. The old man said stop, when he had enough. The old man smiled as he looked at Adam, "Come again. I enjoyed that."

Adam wasn't sure what to say. "That depends on Mum and Dad. It is getting late and I should be getting home."

"I'll see you again," said the old man. They waved to each other.

Mary came to the front of the old people's home. "Hi Mum. Err how did you know I was here?"

"John went home fifteen minutes ago. I was told you were very busy reading the newspaper to one of the old people. I wanted to see it for myself. I know you don't like reading."

Adam blushed. "I didn't know how to say no to the old man. So, I read the newspaper."

"That is so nice of you. How did you find reading the newspaper?"

"Hard at first but easier as I went along. The old man was a good listener and he helped me with some words."

Later that night, Adam told Evette what he had done and that the old man wanted him to go back to read more. "We can do it together," suggested Evette.

"What shock people into thinking we are doing something useful instead of being brats? That's what they all thing of us, brats."

"Yeah. I know. The people can think what they like. They don't have an egg or a piece of paper watching over them. Gee. They would think we are nuts saying that. An egg and a paper watching over us. Gee it sounds stupid just saying it."

"We still have to go to the national park for the final task," said Adam. "Only then will we be free of the egg and paper. Gee it does sound stupid."

It was coming to the end of the month, Adam and Evette were getting worried. The final task wouldn't be completed, and they feared what bad thing would happen. "We have to make a plan," said Adam.

"I have ten dollars left," said Evette.

"That won't be enough," said Adam. "It's fifteen dollars for both of us. We won't have time to earn enough money."

"Just suppose we skipped school. Sports day is coming up and we get our grandparents to take us there instead?"

"We can try," said Adam who wasn't sounding hopeful.

At Westpit, the children waited with their grandparents to catch the ferry to the national park. The ride over was only twenty minutes. They went through the gates to the waiting tour guide.

The guide introduced himself and led everyone to a waiting minibus. The bus took them up to the first lookout. When all the adults were looking around at the view, the twins were looking at the dirt. It was brown, not black. The stones were grey, white and brown.

At the next stop had a picnic area. Everyone ate the prepared food the guide gave them. They were told of different short walk tracks to other lookouts. As they walked with their grandparents, the twins looked at the ground. Red dirt. Brown dirt. White stones. Blueish stones. Reddish stones. And more white stones. Adam sat on the ground at the lookout. He whispered, "We will never finish the task. We are done for." As he was saying this, he played with the brown dirt. Then he noticed something. The black dirt was hiding under the brown. "Get the plastic bag out. Quickly," he whispered to Evette.

Evette pulled a plastic bag out from her pocket. Adam shoved as much dirt into in as he could.
While he tried cleaning his hands up, Evette tied the bag and shoved it in her backpack. There was a call. The guide was going to take them to the last stop of the day.

The bus wound its way up the mountain to the snow line. People took out their cardigans.

The guide said, "We are just below one of the mythical white dragon's spines." Then he added, "You can walk around but be back at the bus in thirty minutes."
The grandfather said to the twins, "That makes it two thirty. Don't go walking where we can't see you." The twins nodded.

Like other children they played in the snow for a short time. Evette didn't notice she was slowly moving backwards towards a small ledge.

She slipped and stumbled down the short slope. She screamed as her stomach scrapped the ground. On the way down she grabbed a stunted bush. She looked down and screamed more. There was a big drop. She pulled herself up. She sat on the small ledge lower down from where she slipped. She screamed for help. By then nearly all the people on tour could see she was stuck. The guide rushed to the bus and pulled out ropes and harnesses.

Evette could hear everyone yelling to stay put and to be clam. Evette gave them a wave and sat down. She looked across over the valley below. She smiled, *Black rocks. Too big*. She looked around the ground she was sitting on. Near the bush she nearly pulled out while she hung on and pulled herself up, she saw some black stones. She shoved four stones into her cardigan pocket and zipped it up.

The guide was soon helping her up. "Gee, how lucky you were. Good thinking grabbing onto that bush." The guide looked at the drop. "Looks like you have some muscles pulling yourself up by using that bush."

"If I had a trowel, I could have made some steps or footholds to the top. I done that before," said Evette.

The guide looked at her. "You don't appear to be scared of heights."

"Not knowing how far I would fall was scarier," replied Evette. "I am still in one piece. My tummy is a bit sore and scratched but that is all. Just some scrapes."

"We will have a look at them when we get to the top. Now, do as I say to get you back to the top." He handed Evette a rope after placing a harness on her. The bus driver will pull you up first. Evette did as she was told but just about ran up the slope all by herself.

She ran to her grandparents and to Adam. The grandparents thanked the guide and the bus driver. On the way back, Evette whispered, "While sitting on that ledge, I found black stones. I have four of them."

Adam gave her a hug. "We just might get the bronze egg and that paper to stop watching us."

At the cubby house, Adam opened the magic box. He presented the dirt and the black stones. The bronze egg split to let the paper out. Again, the paper glowed, and words appeared.

"You have been successful. Here is your reward." The paper turned to go back into an egg. The egg broke open. Four marbles appeared. "Four marbles?" exclaimed Adam." Just Four marbles!"

The egg spoke again, "You are not done with us yet. You will need these for the next two tasks with the silver egg." Evette cried in frustration. "You have to be kidding. We have to work for the silver egg as well? Not fair. You didn't say anything about doing tasks for the silver egg. We are not doing it! "

Glitter swirled around. The children were turned into mules. Both tried to scream but a brayed instead. "Turn us back to children," demand Adam.

The egg spoke, "You two are very stubborn like mules. You must promise to do the two tasks for the silver egg or you will remain that way."

Seeing they had no choice, the twins softly brayed, "We promise."

The glitter swirled around again. The twins were back to normal.

Chapter 9

The silver egg shone brighter than the bronze egg. This time when the silver egg split open smoke came out. It formed into a shape of a man wearing a suit with tails and a top hat. The ghostly man said, "Take two marbles each. Use them to do good. You will receive a reward for doing good. If you do something bad, bad things will happen to you. This time you select a task. You cannot repeat any tasks done at the bronze level."

The man lost his shape and went back inside the egg. The silver egg stopped glowing. The twins locked the eggs away in the box.

Adam sat on the floor feeling very angry. "We should take the eggs back. Our life has been hell."

"Not to mention our reputation is being ruined. Before people were scared of us. Now they think we are goodie goodies. Ugh." Evette sat on the floor with a scowl on her face.

There was a knock on the door. Their grandfather came in. "Are you two okay? I thought I heard some very strange noises coming from in here. It sounded like a man's voice and certainly one like a donkey."

Adam looked up to his grandfather. "We are okay. Nothing wrong. We were having a competition between ourselves as to who could make the most realistic and loudest sound," lied Adam.

"Well it was very loud and very realistic," said the grandfather. "Can you do it again?"

Evette said, "No. It wore us out. Adam won." The grandfather walked away chucking to himself, *They wore themselves out by making animal noises, That's a new one.*

"What are we going to do?" asked Adam when he thought their grandfather was well away from the cubby house.

Evette shrugged. "I don't know. We have to think about doing something good. Something different. But what?"

They sat in silence for a few minutes.

"How about we go for a swim at the beach," suggested Adam. "John and his sister, Tanya, might be there. John told me there might go to the beach today."

"Okay. Grandma may want to come to watch us. We are not supposed to be in the water without an adult around. She might go back if John's parents are there."

At the beach, Adam and Evette met up with John, Tanya and their mother, Ellen. Their grandmother Sally introduced herself to Ellen. Sally decided to stay and chat with Ellen while having an eye on the children. Evette was playing with John's sister Tanya, when a motorboat zoomed past much too close to all swimmers. Tanya disappeared. Evette yelled out, "Tanya! Tanya!." She screamed louder to attract attention of the women on the beach. "Tanya! Tanya! Where are you? Help! Tanya is missing!"

By now Ellen and Sally were in the water looking for Tanya. John and Adam stopped playing and were looking around. Adam yelled, "Over here. She's over here!" Adam swam over to Tanya who was face down in the water and bleeding from the forehead. He flipped her over, held her up the best he could and tried to give her air. Ellen reached Tanya who was starting to look blue. Ellen began resuscitation while walking her back to the beach. Sally called an ambulance. John, Evette and Adam got out of the water and showed concern for Tanya. Evette said, "It was a motor boat speeding fast and too close. Tanya, Tanya! Wake up!"

Tanya started to cough up water. She looked around to see her mother leaning over her. She felt her mother hug her.

She looked at Evette and said, "The boat didn't hit me, but the big splashes did. They pushed me under." Tanya touched her bleeding head. "I didn't know there were rocks under the water. Big black sharp rocks." John, Ellen and Tanya went to the island hospital in an ambulance.

"Well that was the end of that swim," said Adam. "I hope she is alright. That bump on her head was big. I saw the man's face. it was the same man who police think robbed the bank. I bet he's looking to rob something again."

When the twins were back at their grandparents' home, and having afternoon tea, their grandmother, she said, "Adam, that was a brave thing you did: turning Tanya over and trying to give her some air. You tried very hard to pull her to safety. You are a brave boy."
"Shh. Don't tell anyone. It will be embarrassing," said Adam as he reached for a glass of milk.
"Why on Dagon's Lair would it be embarrassing?'
"I am always…and Evette too, are always in trouble at school for being mean. Helping to save someone would wreck that."

The grandmother laughed. "But you two have been doing so many nice things for others over the last few months. I think people are changing their minds or just see you two growing up to be really good citizens."

The twins rolled their eyes and said simultaneously, "Really."

Evette said, "We have to do something about that. When are the police coming?"

"Soon. There was another robbery at a jewellery store. They are attending to that. Adam did you see which way the robber went in the boat?"

"He went passed the jetty to the mainland. That is all. Evette's screaming made me look away from the boat."

"Yeah. The wave from the boat pushed me under. Poor Tanya. I hope she is okay. That bump didn't look nice."

The twins were in the cubby house again. This time they were in Evette's side. "I wonder if that counted as something good? You know finding Tanya so quickly and flipping her over and giving her air."

"I doubt it. Those eggs have a strange twist on rules. If we do something good, then nothing happens. If we say no, then we cop it well and truly."

There was a puff of wind and smoke filled Evette's side of cubby house. The smoke formed into a ghostly shape of the same man with a black suit and top hat. The twins huddled into a corner.

"This time, I am the one watching over you as you do the tasks." The twins just stared with their mouth opened not sure what to think. "The attempt to save Tanya, was good. Good enough for me to say you passed the test. Unfortunately, the rules say you must use the marbles. Consider it a bonus. And here are your bonuses."

He waved his arms around which had formed while he was speaking. The twins each received a ten dollar note. "Your reward." Adam took his very slowly as if it would disappear from his hands. Evette slowly took hers. "Is it going to change in value?" she asked softly knowing the last time she was given money, it changed in value.

"No. This is a magic ten dollar note. When you spend it once, another will reappear. This happens three times. Use it wisely." The smoky image of the man disappeared and went back to the silver egg.

Adam looked at the money. "They always have a catch to anything they give." He stuffed the note into his pocket. Dad will be coming soon. We better get back to the house."

The next morning at school, John met up with Adam. "Thank you for helping my sister. She is at home now. Mum is watching her just in case there is a problem. Do you want to come with me to the shops this afternoon? I want to buy Tanya a fluffy toy."

"Yeah. Evette is having a play over at Jane's house," said Adam.

While they were in the shop, John picked out a monkey. Adam picked out a yellow teddy. He placed it on the counter. Both boys were about to get their wallets out when two men holding guns rushed in. Adam and John froze. The shop assistant went white in the face as he opened the cash register. The shop assistant handed over the cash in the till. The men ran out of the shop.

Adam and John followed. Adam took out his two marbles and rolled them down the street. The marbles multiplied and zoomed much further than either Adam or John could have imagined. The marbles rolled under the men's feet. They slipped and fell backwards to fall heavily on the footpath. THUMP! The money bag they were holding fell to the ground. The shop assistant caught up and with the help of other adults, sat on the men.

John and Adam watched the police cuff the men. When the police finished talking to the surrounding adults, they approached John and Adam. John said, "It was Adam who made them slip by rolling marbles down the footpath." John and Adam went to collect the marbles. None were found.

John looked confused. "I saw a lot of marbles roll down the street. Where did they go?"

"Maybe down the stormwater drain," suggested Adam who had hunch the marbles were back in the bronze egg. They looked down the drain. One policeman looked down as well. None could be seen.

The boys went back to the shop, but the shop assistant had the sign up saying the shop was closed.

Later that evening, Adam told Evette what had happened. He said, "My two marbles have gone. Have you got yours?" Evette nodded. "Still two. I hope I never have to use them like you did. That was really smart and fast thinking." Adam laughed. "You should have seen them; legs and arms flying everywhere. And then bang! Their heads hit the ground. They each must have a giant headache. I bet they have a bigger headache than Tanya. I bet the cops come around again. They are becoming regular visitors here."

"I just hope we don't have to help catch criminals to make my marbles go away. I will be holding mine forever."

A month went by, Evette still had her marbles in her pocket. When she walked down the street, she held them in her hands and jiggled them around inside her pocket. They were always with her. She wondered if she and Adam would ever get rid of the eggs and their tasks they had to do.

It was Saturday morning, their parents were taking them to the mainland to go to the movies. The twins were excited. They didn't go to the mainland that much. It was always nice to get away from Dragon's Lair.

After the movies, their father told them they were in for a surprise. "We are going to a fair and staying late to see the fireworks." The twins enjoyed the fireworks. Their father told them which ones he helped to make. That made it more exciting.

They were going back to the car when they saw a man and a woman on a motor bike zoom through the crowd. People scattered everywhere. As the they drove through the crowd, the lady reached over to snatch ladies' handbags. She had already collected three.

They drove erratically around scaring people as a distraction. That was when the lady swooped and stole bags. The security men were on their communication systems giving each other directions while the police were coming. Like other people, the Smith family ran for cover.

Evette tossed her two marbles. The marbles multiplied and chased the motorbike riders. The marbles went under the tyres of the motorbike. The bike skidded and flipped the riders into their air. All came crashing down with the lady colliding with Evette. Evette was on the ground and pinned down by the now furious lady. The lady stood up and grabbed Evette. Evette was now a shield as the police came running with pointed guns and tasers.

Mary and Tom froze at seeing Evette being used in such a way. Adam yelled out, "Marbles help Evette!" Tom and Mary looked at Adam. Tom was about to say what an unusual thing to say when a cloud of marbles formed a tornado to bombard the thieving couple. Evette ducked when the marbles attacked the lady. Evette crawled away yelling, "Thank you. Thank you for the help!" She ran to Adam and to her parents.

Tom looked at Adam, "You have some explaining to do. What was that?"

"Evette and I found these magic marbles," lied Adam. "It took us a while to work out what they did and how to use them."

"And just how long have you had them?"

Adam shrugged. "A while." He was about to say more when a policeman walked over. It was the same policeman who arrested the store robbers. The policeman recognised Adam.

"Adam?" said the policeman as he recognised Adam. Adam nodded.

"Those marbles you have, exactly where did you get them?"

"Evette and I found only four of them. We discovered when they were used for good, they stopped robbers. But if you did bad things, they attacked. There was a note with them. It said we could only use them two times and then they disappear forever. We don't know where they disappear to," said Adam knowing he was mixing truth with lies. He added, "We will never see them again. They're gone forever."

The policeman looked at Adam with some scepticism. He looked at Evette. "Are you okay?"

Evette nodded. "Never better." She gave a smile that said I am okay, really okay.

Two days later, they were in the cubby house again. Adam said as he pulled out the box with the eggs. "The marbles are gone. We are free of the silver egg."

"Yeah, I wonder what surprises the gold egg has installed for us."

The silver egg shone and spoke in a voice that was close to normal. "You did very well. Now your reward. Lean forward." The smoky man appeared. There was a puff of wind and a sprinkle of glitter. The man said, "Now my sweet young lady, you seem to be a bit accident prone. From now on, you will be protected from bad things happening to you on the condition, you do good things for other people. And as an extra, I give you the gift of being a talented artist and a gifted sportsperson. That is a gift no one can take away from you but yourself. Do bad things and your talent will fade." Evette looked at the magician. She was about to say something, but she changed her mind. She didn't want to know what animal she and Adam would change into if she questioned the reward.

The man looked at Adam. "Hmm. Now let's see. You are not doing so well at school. Your reading has improved because you read to an old man at the nursing home. But we still have a way to go and your maths isn't that great. I will give you the gift of being an excellent student in maths, science and English. Then it is up to you as to what you do with the new talent. Just like your sister, if you do bad things, you will find learning difficult, much more than ever before." The man disappeared by slipping into the silver egg.

Chapter 10

The golden egg glowed and spoke directly to the twins. Its voice was deep, almost like a drum.

"This time you must return items which are not yours to keep. The first is the bag of hidden jewellery. The second is a choice. It is to return the two ten dollar notes or the box. The final one is to return us to our home behind the chest. Everything must be done in that order." The gold egg stopped talking.

Adam and Evette walked to the small cave where Evette had buried her old backpack containing the jewellery. It was almost a year since they first buried the backpack. They wondered what state it would be in. They dug with their trowel until they reached the bag. Adam pulled it out. "Okay, what do we do with it now?"

Evette shrugged. "Give it to the cops. They can find the owner."

They walked into the police station explaining the bag and its contents. The policeman who was starting to know them asked them to go to his office. While they waited, he called their mother and told her what the children had found close to a year ago.

Mary was with the children and heard their story. Evette tipped the contents onto the desk. Everyone looked at the haul. The police photographed each piece before packing each item away.

Days later, the police were at the Smith's home again. The policeman who they spoke to at the station said, "The jeweller identified all the missing items but one. He said it was not his. He told us to give this ring to you. He says thank you."

Evette took the ring and looked at it. "I think it was the first item I found in the sand. Thank you. Can you tell the jeweller we are sorry for keeping his jewellery hidden for so long. Tell him thank you." The policeman nodded. "Now you two keep out of trouble. If you find any magic marbles, let us know." The policeman tilted his hat and walked out of the house.

Evette and Adam looked at the ring. Their mother said, "You have a job to do."

"What's that?" asked Evette.

"Clean the dirt off the ring. I will show you how to do it carefully."

Evette watched her mother use an old toothbrush and give gentle strokes under running water. Evette nodded. "I can do this now," she said confidently. Her mother left the room. Evette gently scrubbed the ring. When all the dirt was off, she smiled. Inside the ring was the same ancient script.

She asked Adam, "Guess what?"

"What?"

"The ring has the ancient script inside it," said Evette. Adam looked at the ring. "Put it away or give it to the eggs. I don't want to start all over again."

When they were at the cubby house a few days later, Adam and Evette decided to return the magical ten dollar notes and keep the box.

They placed the eggs in a backpack along with the ten dollar notes, the coin that was hidden in a jar behind the moveables shelf in Evette's side. Adam placed the key in last. They told their grandfather they were going to the beach to play in the sand.

When they reached the cave, they climbed the footholds they had created almost a year ago. They unlocked the chest of drawers and waited for the chest to swing open. Evette returned the eggs to the nest where she found them. She placed the ten dollar notes around them. Then she added the ring, the old coin and the key.

The key flew out of the nest and into Adam's hand. The ring flew out of the nest and onto Evette's finger. The coin flew out and disappeared. The eggs spoke together, "Thank you and go. Hide the key well. Keep the ring safe. Cover the chest of drawers."

An hour later, the chest was covered in dirt. Adam looked at the key, "Where do we hide this?"
This time the key spoke in a very mechanical type voice. "Not in the dirt again please. I didn't like it there. I liked being in that magic box. I want to live there."

Adam and Evette looked at the magic box in the cubby. He opened up the secret compartment and gasped, "The coin is back here. Look!" Evette looked and gasped. Before she could say anything, the coin spoke. "This is my home. I like it in here. The key can come in. I will like the company." The key flew into the box. "Thank you coin," said the key. The ring which was watching asked, "Can I join you?" The coin and the key looked at the space around them, "Okay. But no more after you. There is no more room." The ring jumped into the box. "Move over key," said the coin.

Adam closed the magic box. Evette said, "Hide the box. I don't want to know where you hide it."
Adam sighed as he looked around. Jokingly he said, "Abracadabra, disappear."
The box flew up into the air and went invisible. Adam and Evette gasped. Adam said, "Abracadabra reappear." The box reappeared. The box said, "Make up your mind."
"Abracadabra disappear." The box disappeared again.

Printed in the USA
CPSIA information can be obtained
at www.ICGtesting.com
LVHW061448190923
758538LV00003BA/94